IRRITATING
—IRMA—

**By Robin Klein • Illustrated by Chris Johnston
and Rowena Cory**

Irma was very good at climbing. Her parents were calm people, who, if they saw Irma clamber up a church steeple or the outside of a lighthouse, would just murmur admiringly, "Lovely, darling." So when they took a vacation cottage near some steep cliffs and Irma told them she was going looking for eagles, they just said, "Lovely, darling."

Irma began to climb the cliffs and halfway up she found a
little door. The door belonged to a dragon who was taking a
very nice long nap, and he wasn't a bit pleased to be woken up.
He stared at Irma's braces and glasses, and he wasn't very
impressed. He rumbled like a forge.

"What a cute green lizard!" said Irma.

The dragon, insulted, uttered a huge echoey roar which splintered granite flakes from his cave.

"That's a nasty cough you've got," said Irma.

The dragon eyed her Spiderman T-shirt and torn jeans and the cap that she had gotten free from a service station. He remembered clearly that maidens usually wore dear little gold crowns and embroidered slippers, and they always squealed when they met him and looked ill at ease. He glared at Irma and spurted forth a long, smoky, orange flame.

"No wonder you've got a cough," Irma said. "Smoking's a nasty habit and bad for your health. And this cave certainly is musty and it needs airing."

The dragon made a noise like bacon frying, but Irma was busy inspecting everything. "You need a broom for a start," she said. "And maybe a cuckoo clock up there by the door. Tsk! Just look at the dust on everything! Tomorrow I'll bring some cleaning equipment and anything else I can think of."

When she left, the dragon set to work, only he didn't do any dusting. He collected boulders and filled up the cave entrance. Bouldered up, and fortressed up, and buttressed up, he smiled grimly to himself and went back to sleep.

Some hours later he woke to a whirring, headachy rumbling. Granite chips rattled around his ears, and Irma scrambled in, carrying a pneumatic power drill. "Good morning," she called. "There must have been a landslide during the night. But I cleaned it up."

The dragon's scales rattled. Angry little flames flickered in his jaw. He made a noise like a hundred barbecues and he squinted ferociously at Irma.

"Don't frown like that," she ordered, tying on an apron. "You'll end up with ugly worry lines. There's a lot of work to get through this morning. First I'll sweep this gritty sand away, and you could really do with a nice carpet in here, or maybe tiles would be better. If there's one thing I just can't stand, it's disorder."

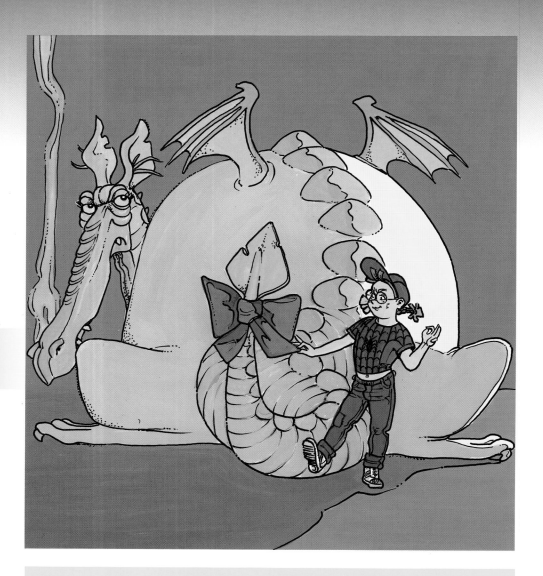

The dragon sizzled fretfully, but worse was to come. When Irma finished cleaning up, she turned her attention to him. She bossily trimmed and lacquered his claws. She polished his scales and lifted up his wings and dusted under them with talcum powder. The dragon blushed but Irma didn't take any notice, because she was busy tying a blue ribbon around his tail. "I've got to be going now," she said. "But I'll be back tomorrow."

The dragon watched her climb down the cliff. "There's only one way to get any peace," he thought. "I'll just have to eat her tomorrow. Freckles will taste nasty, and so will red hair, but maybe if I shut my eyes and gulp, it won't be so bad." He groaned. Parents, he knew from past experience, usually came looking for devoured maidens, waving lances, and acting very unfriendly.

When Irma arrived next morning, he opened his jaws
without much enthusiasm, ready to eat her, but Irma said,
"Look what I brought you!"

She shoved a plate under his nose. On it was a layer cake filled with strawberry cream, iced with chocolate, and covered with sugary pink meringues. The dragon shuddered weakly and felt ill.

"You look as though you're coming down with the flu," said Irma. She took his temperature and spread a blanket over him. The blanket was fluffily pink and edged with satin binding, and the dragon thought it was very babyish.

Irma wrapped it around him and fastened it with a kitten brooch. "I'll leave you to get some rest now, you poor old thing," she said.

"You will?" thought the dragon hopefully.

"But I'll drop by first thing tomorrow," said Irma. "It's lucky for you I still have three weeks of my vacation left.

And every day for three weeks she came, and the dragon suffered. She decorated his cave with potted plants and cushions, a beanbag chair, posters, a bookcase, calendars, and a dart board. She even brought along a toothbrush and bullied him into brushing his teeth.

But at last one morning she said, "I've got to go back to
school tomorrow. You'll just have to look after yourself until
next summer vacation.

When Irma left, the dragon purred and capered about the cave. "Hooray!" he thought. "Good riddance!"

"No more boring chatter and no more being organized, and best of all, undisturbed sleep!" He curled up and shut his eyes.

But his dreams were fretful, and he got up at daybreak feeling grouchy and crabby. He paced his cave and wondered why the silence seemed weary and the hours bleak and long.

He brooded, and nibbled at a claw, and crouched in his doorway staring down at the beach, but it was empty. All the vacation people had gone. Irma had gone.

"Hooray!" he roared. "And she won't be back for many glorious months!"

But why, he wondered glumly, were tears rolling down his cheeks?

Everywhere he looked in his cave he saw things Irma had lugged up the cliff to decorate his cave without permission.

"Yuk," said the dragon morosely, and he kicked a potted plant over the cliff. A wave snatched at it, and the dragon gave a roar of anger and slithered down the cliff and grabbed it back. He carried it crabbily back to his cave and plonked it down on Irma's bookcase.

"Even when she's not here, she's irritating," he thought. "I should have eaten her and gotten it over with. And the very next time I see her, irritating Irma will be my next meal! Freckles and all! Just wait!"

And he waited, but all his little flames flickered out one by one, and his scales lost their sparkle, and his ribboned tail drooped listlessly.

Winter howled through his cave, and he brooded and led a horrid, bad-tempered life.

At last, colored umbrellas began to blossom like flowers along the beach, and it was summer. The dragon sharpened his teeth against the rocks and tried to work up an appetite. And the day came when Irma bounced in through his door, and the indignant dragon opened his massive jaws wide.

"Hello!" cried Irma. "I meant to write, but I forgot your address. Just look what I brought you! Suntan lotion, and a yo-yo with a long string so it will reach down to the bottom of the cliff, and a kite with a picture of you on it, and now tell me, did you miss me? I certainly missed you!"

The dragon blinked in despair at her tangly braids and glasses and braces. "She's talkative and tedious and her manners are terrible!" he reminded himself fiercely.

("And yet," he thought, "it's strange, but I rather like her face.")

"Nonsense!" he roared to himself. "She's annoying and bossy and an utter little nuisance, and no one invited her here; she just walks in as though she owns this whole cliff!"

("And yet," he thought, "of all the maidens all forlorn, I rather like her best.")

"Didn't you miss me?" demanded Irma.

The dragon began to shake his head indignantly, but try as he might to prevent it, the headshake turned into a nod.

"Then we'll celebrate," said Irma. "What would you like for lunch?"

"Plain pancakes, please, Irma," said the dragon.